ONE SMART SHEEP

ONE
SMART
SHEEP

by Gary D. Schmidt and Elizabeth Stickney
with illustrations by Jane Manning

CLARION BOOKS
Houghton Mifflin Harcourt
Boston   New York

Clarion Books
3 Park Avenue
New York, New York 10016

Clarion Books is an imprint of Houghton Mifflin Harcourt Publishing Company.

hmhbooks.com

The illustrations in this book were done in Watercolor and pencil
on Lanaquarelle watercolor paper.
The text was set in Kepler Std.
Cover design by Kaitlin Yang
Interior design by Andrea Miller

Library of Congress Cataloging-in-Publication Data is available.
ISBN 978-0-544-88835-7

Manufactured in China
SCP 10 9 8 7 6 5 4 3 2 1
4500826705

For Carolyn and Samantha,
with all my love

—G.D.S.

For Jean, with love

—J.M.

CHAPTER ONE

On Atwood Hill

Wilson was Abigail Atwood's friendliest sheep.

Wilson was Abigail Atwood's woolliest sheep.

And Wilson was Abigail Atwood's smartest sheep.

That is a lot for one sheep to be.

Every morning, Wilson waited for Abigail to climb the stony path that led from her little red house to the sheep pen and the pasture at the top of Atwood Hill.

And every morning, Wilson waited for Tippy, Abigail's faithful and obedient Border collie, who always came right behind her.

"Good morning, Wilson," Abigail Atwood always said.

"Baa," Wilson would say, and then Abigail Atwood would open the gate from the sheep pen to the pasture, and twenty-six sheep would crowd through. None of them ever stopped on the way to the thick grass.

Except Wilson, the twenty-seventh sheep.

Wilson always stopped, because he was friendly. He would rub his woolly head against Abigail's knee. Then—and Abigail Atwood was sure he did this—Wilson would wink at her.

When he did that, Abigail always bent down and patted him.

"How's my friendliest, woolliest, smartest sheep today?" Abigail would ask.

Wilson would look up at Abigail.

"Baa," he would say.

Then Abigail would always scratch under Wilson's chin. And Wilson would always close his eyes with happiness.

"Be a good sheep today," Abigail would say, and Tippy would touch noses with Wilson, and Abigail would close the pasture gate and check the latch. Then they would walk down the stony path and turn toward the little red house, Abigail in front, Tippy close behind.

And Wilson would watch them and think about Abigail on her front porch, patting Tippy's black-and-white head before they went inside to the warm woodstove, where Tippy's tail would thwack thwack thwack on the wood floor and Abigail's rocking chair would creak creak creak back and forth.

And Wilson would bleat a soft baa that was a little bit lonely.

CHAPTER TWO

Neighbors

Abigail Atwood had one neighbor on Atwood Hill: Jeremiah Jefferson. Jeremiah Jefferson always brought a proper cap with him whenever he left the house. "It is what you do," he said. And he always carried three screwdrivers, a couple of socket wrenches, and a pair of pliers in his back pocket. "You never know when you might need your tools," he said. And he needed his tools all the time, because he fixed pickup trucks and tractors and rototillers and lawn mowers and anything else that rolled on wheels—

especially if what rolled on wheels had an engine that made very loud noises.

Abigail Atwood and Tippy did not care for very loud noises.

Jeremiah Jefferson did not care for sheep.

"Sheep are stupid as all get-out," said Jeremiah Jefferson this morning as he pumped a little more air into the plump tires of Abigail's quiet bicycle.

Abigail Atwood cleared her throat.

"They'd follow each other over a cliff, given half a chance," said Jeremiah Jefferson as he adjusted the bicycle's brakes.

Abigail Atwood cleared her throat again.

"And probably get lost on the way down," said Jeremiah Jefferson as he lowered the bicycle seat a little.

Abigail Atwood stared at Jeremiah Jefferson. "I sometimes wonder if Wilson might be every bit as smart as you are," she said.

"Can he grease a bicycle chain?" asked Jeremiah Jefferson.

Abigail Atwood put her hands on her hips. "Wilson cannot grease a bicycle chain because he has tiny hooves. He can, however, grow a thick coat of wool—which is more than I can say for some."

Jeremiah Jefferson put his cap on his bald head. The air was a little frosty.

"Sheep are ugly," he said.

Tippy's ears went up, and she showed some of her teeth to Jeremiah Jefferson.

"Wilson," said Abigail Atwood, "is not only the friendliest, woolliest, and smartest sheep in the county. He is also the handsomest."

"That so?" said Jeremiah Jefferson.

"Come see for yourself," said Abigail Atwood.

Jeremiah Jefferson followed Abigail Atwood up the stony path toward the pasture,
Tippy right behind them.

When Wilson saw Abigail open the pasture
gate and Tippy waving her tail, he trotted to
them and rubbed his woolly head against
Abigail's knee. She scratched him under his
chin.

"Isn't Wilson a handsome sheep?" said
Abigail.

Jeremiah Jefferson looked at Wilson. Wilson's nose was runny. He had dandelion fluff
in his wool. He was chewing a long strand of

yellow grass that drooped out of his mouth. He was drooling.

"I suppose he'd look handsome to some," said Jeremiah Jefferson.

If Abigail Atwood hadn't given Tippy a very stern look, Tippy might have nipped Jeremiah Jefferson in a place that would have kept him from sitting on a tractor for several days.

But she said to Jeremiah Jefferson, "I wonder if something loud needs fixing back at your house."

"I don't think so," he said.

"You should go home to make sure."

Jeremiah Jefferson walked back home to make sure.

Abigail closed the pasture gate, but she and Tippy were annoyed. As they marched back to the little red house, they were so annoyed that they did not hear Wilson's lonely baa. They did not notice him leaning his woolly head against the gate.

And they did not check the latch.

CHAPTER THREE

Winter Coming

Tippy knew all about sheep. She knew which ones did what they were told and which ones liked to make up their own minds. She knew which ones stayed with the flock and which ones wandered. She knew which ones she had to bark at and which ones she had to nip just a little to get them into the pen at night.

And she knew Wilson was special.

Tippy remembered when Wilson was a tiny lamb and slept wrapped in a checkered quilt in the box by the woodstove. She remembered how Abigail fed him milk from a warm bottle. She remembered how Wilson grew a little bigger and they would lie back to back at night. She remembered how in the mornings, Wilson followed her all over Atwood Hill. He would try to put his ears up and crouch down low the way Border collies do when they herd sheep.

And Tippy remembered the summer afternoon when she stood with Abigail by the open pasture gate, watching the sheep graze, and Wilson stretched his head toward Tippy, and they touched noses, and then Wilson trotted through the gate to join the twenty-six sheep grazing on Atwood Hill.

Abigail had closed the gate and checked

the latch. Then she and Tippy had walked down the stony path back to the little red house, and Tippy was a little bit lonely.

Tippy remembered all of that.

Now, Tippy held her nose up into the wind. She could smell the sheep in the pasture. She could smell Jeremiah Jefferson's loud machines. She could smell the cooler air of early winter.

Tippy lay down and thought about the woodstove.

Abigail Atwood smelled the cooler air of early winter too, and she thought about long, cold nights, and how quiet they could be, and she tried to hum a song about summer and cuckoo birds and ewes.

"Tippy," she said, "do you remember that silly song we sang for Wilson when he was just a lamb?"

Tippy cocked her head and looked at Abigail.

"No, I can't remember it either."

Tippy barked her helpful bark.

Abigail tried again to hum a snatch or two.

Tippy barked her encouraging bark.

"A piano! What a good idea!" Abigail said. "Why didn't we think of it before? A piano is exactly what we need for long winter nights."

So Abigail called the piano store on Sullivan Street. The salesman was very helpful. They had an upright piano in the showroom that would be perfect, the young man said. They could deliver it to Atwood Hill right away. "Would that be convenient?" the young man asked.

"That would be splendid," Abigail Atwood said. "Wouldn't that be splendid, Tippy?"

Tippy barked her happy bark.

CHAPTER FOUR
What Wilson Saw

Standing by the pasture gate, Wilson heard Tippy barking. He said "Baa" and wished he could bark. He tried to put his ears up and crouch down low the way Border collies do. When he stood again, his woolly head hit the gate.

The gate moved.

Wilson was frightened. He trotted to the other side of the pasture, behind the twenty-six other sheep, who were all grazing happily. Wilson watched the gate closely.

He watched it for a long time.

It did not move again.

Wilson went back to the gate. He said "Baa," but the gate did not say anything back. He reached forward and touched it with his nose. Then he butted it with his woolly head.

It moved again.

Wilson trotted back to the other side of the pasture.

He watched the gate closely.

He watched it for a long time.

He thought about Abigail, and Tippy, and the stony path, and the woodstove, and the smell of blueberries in the warm kitchen of the little red house.

Wilson went back to the gate. He butted it with his woolly head.

It moved.

None of the other sheep left their graz-ing when Wilson butted the pasture gate so hard that it opened wide. And none of them left their grazing when Wilson scooted out before the gate swung slowly back.

And none of them saw Wilson trot down the stony path toward the little red house and the piano delivery truck that had just parked in front of it.

CHAPTER FIVE

What Tippy Saw

With one finger on the keyboard, Abigail Atwood tried to play the song about summer and cuckoo birds and ewes. She couldn't make it sound exactly as she remembered.

"Tippy, what am I doing wrong?" Abigail said.

Tippy looked out the window. Her ears were up and her paws were on the sill. She barked.

"Is someone here?" asked Abigail Atwood.

"It's me," called Jeremiah Jefferson.

Abigail got off her new piano bench and

went to the door.

"Couldn't help but notice your new truck," said Jeremiah Jefferson.

"It's not my new truck," said Abigail. "It is a delivery truck from the piano store on Sullivan Street."

Jeremiah Jefferson looked disappointed. "Oh," he said.

"It probably makes a very loud noise," said Abigail.

"Hope so," said Jeremiah Jefferson.

The two deliverymen came in from the kitchen. One had a milk mustache. The other was holding half of a blueberry muffin.

"Thanks, Ms. Atwood."

"Thank *you*," said Abigail. "You may deliver a piano to my house anytime."

"What kind of engine you got under that hood?" asked Jeremiah Jefferson.

The deliverymen looked at each other. They shrugged.

"Sounds like it's idling a little slow," said Jeremiah Johnson.

"Maybe," said one of the deliverymen.

"Let's go find out," said Jeremiah Jefferson. He pulled a socket wrench from his back pocket and they went outside.

Abigail went back to her new piano bench.

"Tippy," she said, "you haven't moved at all. What are you staring at?"

Tippy jumped from the windowsill. She put her ears up and crouched down low. Then she ran back to the windowsill.

She barked her frantic bark.

CHAPTER SIX
What Abigail Did Not See

Wilson stood at the bottom of the ramp that led into the piano delivery truck in front of Abigail Atwood's little red house. He had never seen a path like it before, and he wondered where it led. Then Wilson smelled something. He put his nose in the air—the way Tippy did—and sniffed. Blueberry muffins! He took a step toward the little red house, with its warm kitchen and warm woodstove.

Then Wilson heard a very loud noise coming from the front of the truck.

And he heard Tippy's frantic bark.

With the very loud noise coming from the front of the truck, it was hard for a sheep—even a very smart sheep—to tell where Tippy's frantic bark was coming from.

Wilson looked up the strange path.

The pen at the top of it looked warm and comfortable.

Maybe it had a woodstove.

Maybe that's where Tippy was.

Wilson put one front hoof on the ramp, then the other.

Then he put his two back hooves on the ramp and began to climb.

It took only a few steps to reach the top of the ramp, and Wilson was right: The pen was warm and comfortable. The wood floor was worn smooth. Thick pads lined the walls.

And a yellow light on the ceiling illuminated everything.

He moved farther into the warm pen and looked around.

No Tippy.

No Abigail.

No woodstove, either.

Wilson began to wonder if a friendly, woolly, smart sheep belonged here after all.

Then the two deliverymen lifted the ramp into the truck. Wilson said "Baa," but the deliverymen did not hear Wilson over the very loud noise in front.

The back doors slammed shut. "Baa," said Wilson.

Then the light went out. "Baa, baa," said Wilson.

"You want me to back it up?" Wilson heard Jeremiah Jefferson ask.

Wilson baaed his frantic baa.

"That's okay," said one of the deliverymen.

Tippy began to bark again.

"Baa, baa, baa," said Wilson.

"Thank you, gentlemen," Wilson heard Abigail say. "You've brought music to Atwood Hill."

"Baa, baa, baa, baa," said Wilson.

CHAPTER SEVEN

What Tippy Showed Abigail

When Abigail came out onto the porch to wave goodbye to the deliverymen, Tippy came out with her. Tippy ran to the back of the truck and barked. When the truck drove down Atwood Hill, Tippy ran beside it, barking all the way. When the truck pulled out onto the road and headed into town, Tippy ran back to the little red house and jumped, panting, onto the porch.

"What has gotten into you?" asked Abigail Atwood.

"Looks like she wants to tell you something," said Jeremiah Jefferson.

Tippy turned three times in a circle and looked at Abigail.

"It will have to wait," said Abigail.

Tippy put her ears up and crouched down low.

"Certainly not," said Abigail. "We were up to the pasture this morning."

Tippy whined.

"Sure does look like she wants something," said Jeremiah Jefferson. "A blueberry muffin maybe?"

Abigail Atwood looked at Jeremiah Jefferson. "You're sure that's what *she* wants?" she said.

"Pretty sure," said Jeremiah Jefferson.

Abigail Atwood went inside her little red

house and came out with three blueberry muffins. She handed them to Jeremiah Jefferson.

"I was talking about the dog," said Jeremiah Jefferson.

"Of course," said Abigail. She waved goodbye to Jeremiah Jefferson and opened the door to the little red house. She went inside with Tippy and sat on her new piano bench. She played a few scales, then tried to pick out the song about summer and cuckoo birds and ewes. This time she got it just right.

"Did you hear that, Tippy?" said Abigail.

Tippy whined.

Abigail was losing patience with Tippy. "What is it?" she asked.

Tippy put her ears up and crouched down low.

"Now?" she said.

Tippy crouched down even lower.

"All right, all right," said Abigail. She went to the closet and put on her coat. "Let's go."

Abigail and Tippy climbed up the stony path toward the pasture. Tippy ran ahead, then came back, ran ahead, came back, ran ahead, came back—her tail waving in circles.

"Honestly," said Abigail.

When they reached the pasture, the sheep were grazing—as they always were. Abigail counted them, just to be sure. "Twenty-four, twenty-five, twenty-six. You see, Tippy, they're all . . . Wait a moment."

Abigail put her hand on the pasture gate. It swung open easily.

"Oh, mercy," said Abigail.

CHAPTER EIGHT

What Would Tippy Do?

In the back of the piano delivery truck, Wilson tried to be brave. But it is hard for a sheep—even a very friendly, woolly, smart sheep—to stand bravely in the back of a piano delivery truck.

Whenever the deliveryman stepped on the brakes, Wilson slid forward into the pads at the front of the truck. When the deliveryman stepped on the accelerator, Wilson slid into the back doors. When the deliveryman took a right-hand turn, Wilson skidded into the pads on the left wall. When the deliveryman

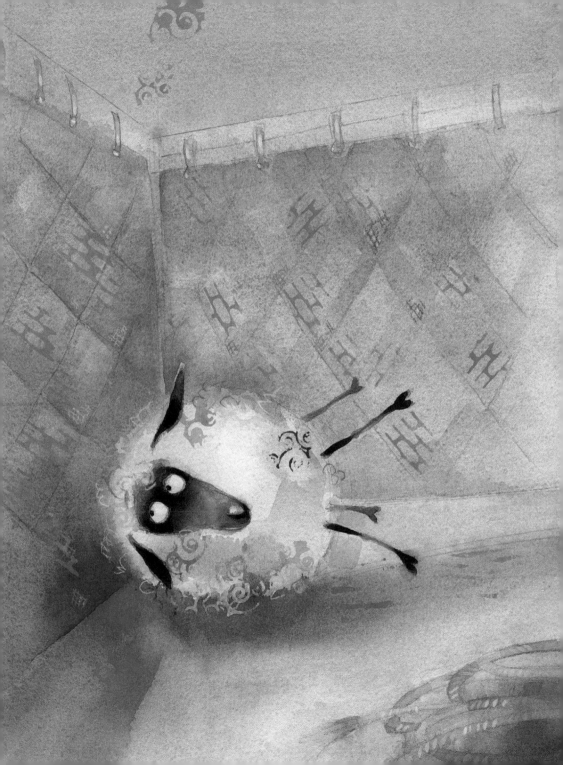

took a left turn, Wilson skidded into the pads on the right wall.

It wasn't long before Wilson gave up trying to be brave. He huddled in a corner and baa-ed his frantic baa.

But he was alone in the back of the piano delivery truck.

And he was hearing things he had never heard on Atwood Hill: the rumble of trucks hauling heavy loads, a jackhammer pounding. And they were louder than any of Jeremiah Jefferson's machines.

In a little while, the delivery truck slowed down and Wilson heard someone calling "Hot dogs! Hot dogs! Two for a buck!" And he heard a calliope singing breathy music. He had never heard a calliope before. He put his ears up like a Border collie.

Then the delivery truck slowed down even more, and Wilson heard the high, light bells of a church steeple chiming, and the slow, deep bells of a clock tower tolling. He closed his eyes. Wilson had never heard anything so beautiful as these chimes and bells.

As they got close to Sullivan Street, the delivery truck stopped often before it made a turn. Wilson heard cars honking and brakes squealing and sirens passing by.

Wilson stood. He was afraid. He wondered what the sounds he heard meant.

Then Wilson thought about what Tippy would do if she were in the back of the piano delivery truck.

Tippy would not be afraid.

Tippy would wait by the back doors, and when they opened, Tippy would leap out and look for where the sounds came from.

Wilson knew that was exactly what Tippy would do.

So when the truck stopped, Wilson moved to the back doors. He put his ears up and crouched down low the way Border collies do.

He waited for the doors to open.

CHAPTER NINE

High and Low

Abigail counted the sheep one more time. She walked all around the fence and looked over Atwood Hill as far as her sharp eyes could see. She looked in the sheep pen. Then she made her way down the stony path as quickly as she could. She looked to the right and to the left, but Wilson was nowhere in sight. She looked all around the little red house, but no Wilson. She looked on the front porch. She even looked in the kitchen by the woodstove.

No Wilson.

"Tippy, it's almost as if he were taken away," said Abigail—and then she remembered the piano deliverymen and their very loud truck.

And she remembered Tippy's barking.

"Oh, Tippy," Abigail said, "why didn't I listen to you?"

Abigail found her telephone. She dialed the number of the piano store on Sullivan Street. She tried not to imagine what Wilson was going through in the back of the delivery truck.

But when the young man at the piano shop answered the telephone, he was not very helpful.

"A real sheep?" the young man asked.

"Yes," said Abigail.

"A sheep that goes 'baa, baa'?"

"Yes," said Abigail.

"You think there's a real sheep in the back of our truck?" said the young man.

"Yes. A sheep that goes 'baa, baa,'" said Abigail.

"Listen, I don't have time for jokes," said the young man.

"Neither do I," said Abigail. "And this is certainly no joke."

The young man hung up.

"What a rude person," said Abigail to Tippy.

Tippy was standing and looking at Abigail. She barked her worried bark.

"I know," said Abigail. "We will have to find Wilson ourselves, Tippy."

Abigail made her second phone call.

"Mr. Jefferson," she said, "we have an emergency. We need to go to town immediately to find Wilson. If you ever hope to have another blueberry muffin . . ."

"I'll be right over," said Jeremiah Jefferson.

CHAPTER TEN

Wilson's Leap

Wilson felt the delivery truck stop. The loud noise in the front stopped, too. Doors opened and closed. Wilson heard someone singing—the song was not as nice as Abigail's. Then the singing stopped and Wilson heard voices at the back of the truck. He heard the doors unlock.

Wilson's ears were up. He was crouching down low.

When the back doors opened, Wilson said "Baa" as loudly as a sheep can say baa, and he leaped like a Border collie over the heads of the two astonished deliverymen—who made sounds almost as loud as Wilson's—and clattered on his tiny hooves into the parking lot beside the piano store on Sullivan Street.

Wilson turned to the two deliverymen. "Baa," he said. He was trying for Tippy's fierce bark, and he came so close that the two deliverymen ran into the piano store.

"Baa," said Wilson again. This was his satisfied baa, because he was very pleased with himself.

He looked around. Buildings taller than Abigail's little red house reared up on one side. He looked around again. Buildings taller than Atwood Hill reared up on the other side. Beside them, cars sped by, making sounds as loud as Jeremiah Jefferson's machines. Above them, thick gray clouds gathered.

"Baa," said Wilson. This was not his satisfied baa. This was his frightened baa. He wished he were back in the sheep pen at Atwood Hill.

People passing by stopped and pointed at him.

"Baa," said Wilson again. This was his I-am-about-to-cry baa.

Wilson ran out of the parking lot beside the piano store and onto Sullivan Street. There were many more buildings here, and

many more cars, and many more people who pointed at him.

"Baa," said Wilson. This was his I-am-crying baa.

Wilson ran down Sullivan Street. He did not run very fast. Sheep do not run very fast, especially when they have a thick coat of wool to carry and they are baaing their I-am-crying baa.

When Wilson heard a particularly loud machine coming toward him, he turned on to a side street and ran as fast as he could—which still wasn't very fast—on his tiny hooves. He was thirsty. He began to pant because he was out of breath.

"Baa," he said—and it was his lonely baa.

And then Wilson heard a clock begin to toll. He stopped running. He listened. The tolls were slow and deep.

He had heard them before.

He remembered them.

Wilson put his ears up the way Border collies do. He listened. Then, on his tiny hooves, he trotted toward the tolling clock tower.

The thick gray clouds grew darker.

CHAPTER ELEVEN

Sniffing Around

Tippy stretched her nose out of the open window of Jeremiah Jefferson's car. She tried to catch a sniff of Wilson, but town was nothing like Atwood Hill. Tippy smelled diesel fuel and grilled Italian sausages and pepperoni and cooking oil and rubber and dry leaves in the air, and the grease on Jeremiah Jefferson's wrench sticking out of his back pocket. But Tippy did not smell Wilson.

"Why do you always wear that old cap?" yelled Abigail. She had to yell because Jeremiah Jefferson's car was very loud.

"To make me look handsome," hollered Jeremiah Jefferson.

"It's not working," yelled Abigail Atwood.

Jeremiah Jefferson gripped the wheel tightly. The road in town was crowded and busy, nothing like the road by Atwood Hill.

"There." Abigail pointed. "Sullivan Street. We're almost there. Look for the piano shop."

They found it only a block later, and Jeremiah Jefferson parked in front. Abigail and Tippy were out in a moment.

Abigail opened the door and a little bell sounded. "May I help you find a piano today?" the young man asked.

"I have a piano," said Abigail. "I'm looking for a sheep."

"So you're the lady with the sheep," said

the young man.

Abigail was not sure she liked this young man very much.

"Has your delivery truck come back?" she said.

"It has—and your sheep scared the daylights out of our deliverymen."

Tippy was not sure she liked this young man very much either.

"Grown men," said Abigail, "are rarely frightened by sheep. Where is Wilson?"

"Gone," said the young man.

"Gone?" said Abigail.

"Gone," said the young man.

"Gone where?" asked Abigail.

"Gone I have no idea where," said the young man.

If Abigail Atwood hadn't given Tippy a very stern look, Tippy might have nipped the young man in a place that would have kept him from sitting on a piano bench for several days.

Abigail and Tippy went back to Jeremiah Jefferson's car.

"We'll have to drive around town to see if we can find Wilson," yelled Abigail.

Jeremiah Jefferson drove into the traffic. Tippy's nose sniffed the air. Abigail's sharp eyes peered down every street.

Jeremiah Jefferson looked up at the sky. "Looks like snow," he said.

CHAPTER TWELVE

What Wilson Remembered

Wilson stood below the clock tower. Above him, the last bells had finished their slow, deep tolling. He looked around, but he could not see Atwood Hill. Snow in the air fell softly, and Wilson baaed his confused baa.

Then Wilson's ears went up the way Border collies' do.

He heard more bells.

They were high and light, and they were chiming in a steeple not far away.

On his tiny hooves, Wilson trotted toward the church.

Even though he was a friendly sheep, Wilson paid no attention to the people on the sidewalk who looked at him as if they had never seen a sheep heading toward a church before.

He was listening to the light bells.

"Baa," said Wilson.

When he got to the chiming steeple, Wilson looked around. He put his nose in the air—the way Tippy did—and sniffed. He did not smell anything familiar, but from far away, he heard something he remembered: the breathy singing of the calliope. It was very, very faint, and a sheep not quite as smart as Wilson might not have recognized it. But Wilson did, and, on his tiny hooves, he trotted toward the singing calliope.

When he reached it, Wilson was well out of town. The road was no longer crowded with cars honking and brakes squealing and sirens passing by. On one side of the road, all the cars had been chased into a pen and were being quiet, and on the other side of the road a calliope was playing beside a big tent with flags flying on top and lots of people herded inside.

Wilson listened carefully. None of these was the song Abigail used to sing to him on cold nights while he lay under the checkered quilt in the box beside the woodstove in the kitchen.

Then Wilson heard something else. From not very far away, he heard someone calling "Hot dogs! Hot dogs! Two for a buck!"

Wilson trotted to the man who was calling, and the man gave Wilson two hot dog buns with some onions. Wilson ate them quickly. They were not nearly as good as the thick grass of Atwood Hill, but he was hungry.

The man with the hot dogs looked up to the cloudy sky. "You better get on home, sheep," he said, and Wilson thought so too. But which way was Atwood Hill?

Then, from very far away, Wilson heard the sound of a jackhammer pounding pounding pounding. He remembered that sound. On his tiny hooves, he trotted down the road away from town. The snow was falling a little harder now, and it landed on Wilson's wool, and his eyelashes, and his ears—which were up the way Border collies' are.

When he reached the pounding pounding pounding, there was snow on the man holding the jackhammer too. The man took off his glasses and wiped snowflakes from them. And when he put his glasses back on, he saw Wilson. "What are you doing out here?" he said.

"Baa," said Wilson.

But Wilson did not stay to talk. Ahead of him he heard the rumble of trucks hauling heavy loads. He hurried on.

CHAPTER THIRTEEN
Where Is Wilson?

Abigail Atwood, Jeremiah Jefferson, and Tippy drove with heavy hearts. They had driven up and down every street in town. They had gone back to the piano store on Sullivan Street to check the truck once more—just in case. Tippy had sniffed until her nose was almost frozen.

No sign of Wilson at all. Not anywhere.

The tolling of the clock tower told them how late it was getting. Soon it would be dark. And it was starting to snow hard.

"Oh, mercy," yelled Abigail.

"We'll drive down Sullivan Street one more time," hollered Jeremiah Jefferson.

They did.

No Wilson.

"We'd better go home," yelled Abigail. "The other sheep will need tending to."

"We'll look again tomorrow," hollered Jeremiah Jefferson.

"Thank you," yelled Abigail.

They drove toward Atwood Hill. At the edge of town, they passed a circus, where a calliope was singing breathily. Outside the gate, a man was taking down the snowy umbrella over his hot dog stand. "I suppose it's too cold and wet for anyone to buy hot dogs now," yelled Abigail.

They drove farther, and a man was brushing the snow off his jackhammer and putting it away for the night. Ahead of him, trucks rumbled onto the road, carrying heavy loads.

"Those are powerful trucks," hollered Jeremiah Jefferson.

"Yes," yelled Abigail sadly.

Ahead was Atwood Hill. About halfway up, the lights of the little red house glowed.

Then Tippy began to bark.

And bark.

And bark.

"Looks like she wants to tell you something," hollered Jeremiah Johnson.

"What is it, Tippy?" yelled Abigail.

Tippy barked again, then began scratching at the door. She barked her frantic bark.

Jeremiah Jefferson stopped, and when Abigail opened her door, and when Tippy bounded out, and when Abigail got out after her, and when Jeremiah Jefferson got out after Abigail, they all saw the same thing: one friendly, woolly, smart sheep trotting along the side of the road on tiny hooves, covered in snow, and heading toward Atwood Hill.

Wilson.

CHAPTER FOURTEEN

By the Woodstove

Night had come quickly to Atwood Hill. At the top of the hill, twenty-six sheep were safe in their pen. It would be a cold night, and Tippy had snuggled them close together. Then she and Abigail had come down the stony path to the little red house.

Inside, Jeremiah Jefferson had finished stoking the woodstove, and it was warm and glowing happily. Abigail reached into the kitchen cupboard and brought out three blueberry muffins and put them on a plate.

She gave one to Jeremiah Jefferson. "Thank you," she said.

"I didn't do anything," said Jeremiah Jefferson. "Wilson came home all by himself. I have to admit, that sure is one smart sheep."

"And," Abigail said, "you do look handsome when you have that old cap off."

Abigail put the plate on the kitchen table, and then she broke the second blueberry muffin in half. She gave half to Tippy, who lay beside the woodstove, and half to Wilson, who lay beside Tippy.

She patted Tippy's head, then Wilson's. "Just this once," she said.

Then Abigail took the plate with the last blueberry muffin and she set it on her new piano bench, and she put her fingers on the keys and she played her new piano. She played the song about summer and cuckoo birds and ewes, because she remembered it now, and that is how she felt.

Tippy laid her head on the floor and closed her eyes. Wilson laid his head on the floor and closed his eyes, too. It had been a long day and they were sleepy. They listened to the music.

And high above them, the music about summer and cuckoo birds and ewes floated along the stony path and up Atwood Hill. It floated into the sheep pen, where twenty-six sheep lay side by side, their eyes closed, asleep.

Except for Marigold, who was listening to the music. She stood up. She nudged her way past the other twenty-five sheep and woke them. Marigold looked down the stony path toward the little red house. The snow had slowed and the moon was trying to shine all over Atwood Hill.

Marigold went to the sheep pen gate to get a closer look. Then she butted the gate with her woolly head.

It moved.

The other twenty-five sheep stood up behind Marigold.

Marigold butted the sheep pen gate with her woolly head again.

The other twenty-five sheep said, "Baa."

* * *

A little while later, Tippy and Wilson lifted their heads. Tippy barked and Wilson raised his ears up the way Border collies do.

"Is someone here?" asked Abigail, rising from her new piano bench.

She went to the window and looked out into the darkness.

"Who is it?" asked Jeremiah Jefferson.

"Oh, mercy," said Abigail Atwood, and with Tippy the Border collie and Wilson the smart sheep crowding behind her, she opened the door.